The Rich Man and the Shoemaker

For all children, young and old.

OXFORD
UNIVERSITY PRESS

Oxford University Press is a department of the University of Oxford.
It furthers the University's objective of excellence in research, scholarship,
and education by publishing worldwide in

Oxford   New York

Auckland   Cape Town   Dar es Salaam   Hong Kong   Karachi
Kuala Lumpur   Madrid   Melbourne   Mexico City   Nairobi
New Delhi   Shanghai   Taipei   Toronto

With offices in
Argentina   Austria   Brazil   Chile   Czech Republic   France   Greece
Guatemala   Hungary   Italy   Japan   Poland   Portugal   Singapore
South Korea   Switzerland   Thailand   Turkey   Ukraine   Vietnam

Oxford is a registered trade mark of Oxford University Press
in the UK and in certain other countries

First published 1965
First published in paperback 1983
Reissued in paperback 1999
This new edition first published in paperback 2008

British Library Cataloguing in Publication Data
Data available

ISBN: 978-0-19-272090-0 (paperback)

1 3 5 7 9 10 8 6 4 2

Printed in China

Brian Wildsmith

The Rich Man and the Shoemaker

OXFORD
UNIVERSITY PRESS

Once upon a time there lived a *poor*
but *cheerful* shoemaker.

He was *so* happy he *sang* all day long. The children loved to stand round his window to listen to him.

Next door to the shoemaker lived a rich man.

He used to sit up all night to count his gold.

In the morning he went to bed, but he could not sleep because of the sound of the shoemaker's singing.

One day he thought of a way of stopping the singing.

He wrote a letter to the shoemaker asking him to call.

The shoemaker came at once, and *to his surprise* the rich man gave him a bag of gold.

When he got home again, the shoemaker opened the bag.
He had never seen *so much* money before! He sat
down at his bench and began, carefully, to count it.
The children watched through the window.

There was so much there that the shoemaker was afraid to let it out of his sight. So he took it to bed with him.

But he *could not sleep* for worrying about it. So he got out of bed and went to hide it

in the attic, but he was not sure
if that was a good place.

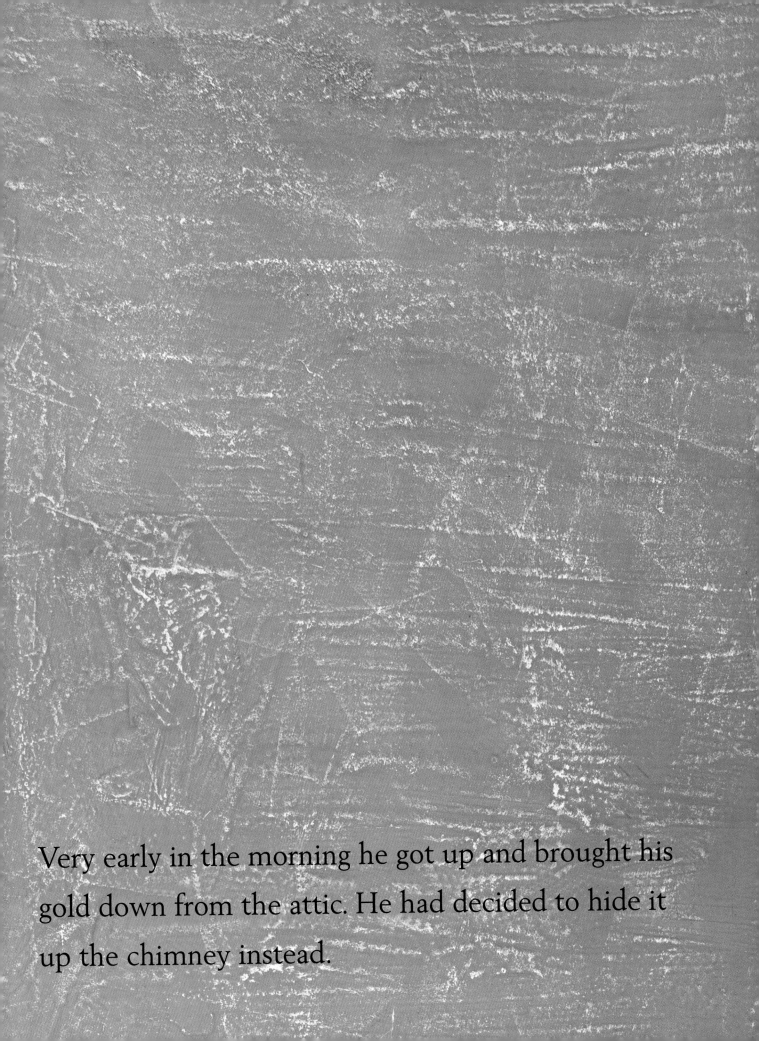

Very early in the morning he got up and brought his gold down from the attic. He had decided to hide it up the chimney instead.

But after breakfast he thought it would be safer in the chicken-house. So he hid it there.

But he was still uneasy and in a little while he dug a
hole in the garden, and buried his bag of gold in it.

It was no use trying to work. He was too worried about the safety of his gold. And as for singing, he was too *miserable* to utter a note. He could not sleep, or work, or sing – and, *worst of all*, the children no longer came to see him.

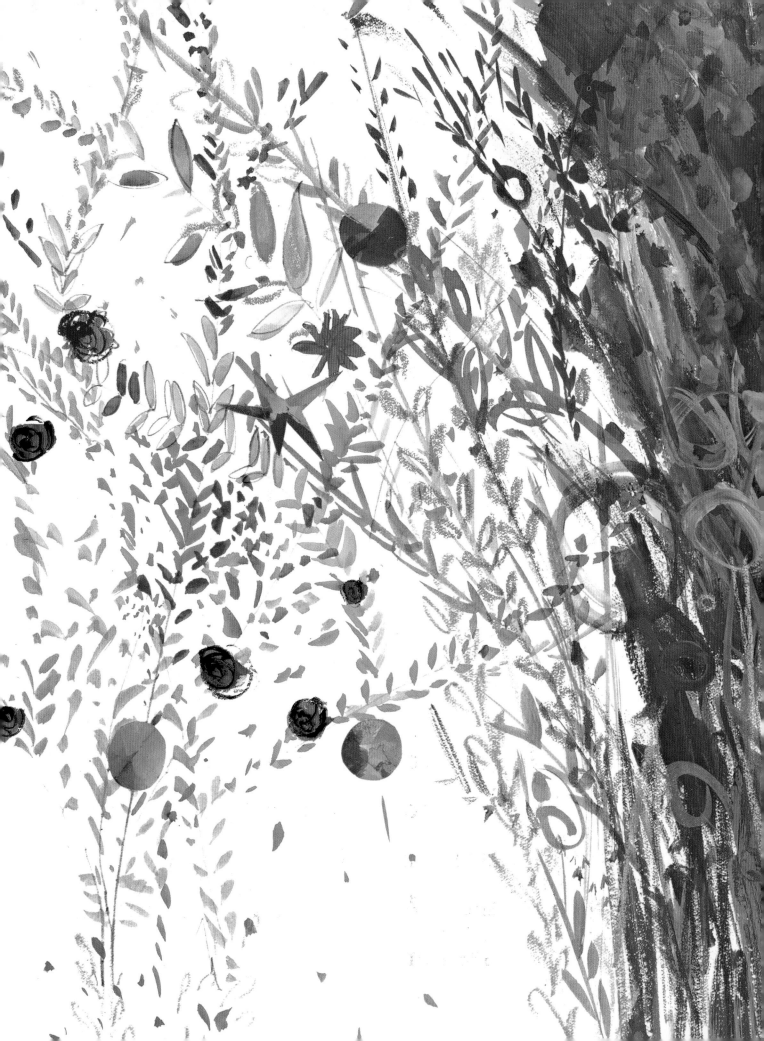

At last the shoemaker
felt so unhappy that
he seized his bag of
gold and ran next
door to the rich man.
'*Please* take back
your gold,' he said.
'The worry of it is
making me *ill* and I
have lost all my friends.
I would rather be a
poor shoemaker,
as I was before.'

And so the shoemaker was *happy* again,
and *sang* all day at his work.